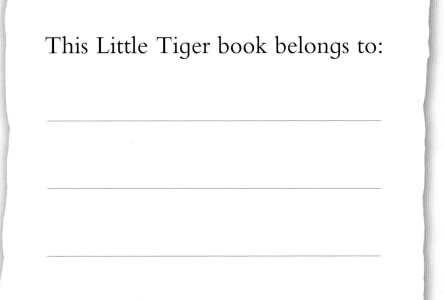

This Little Tiger book belongs to:

_____

_____

_____

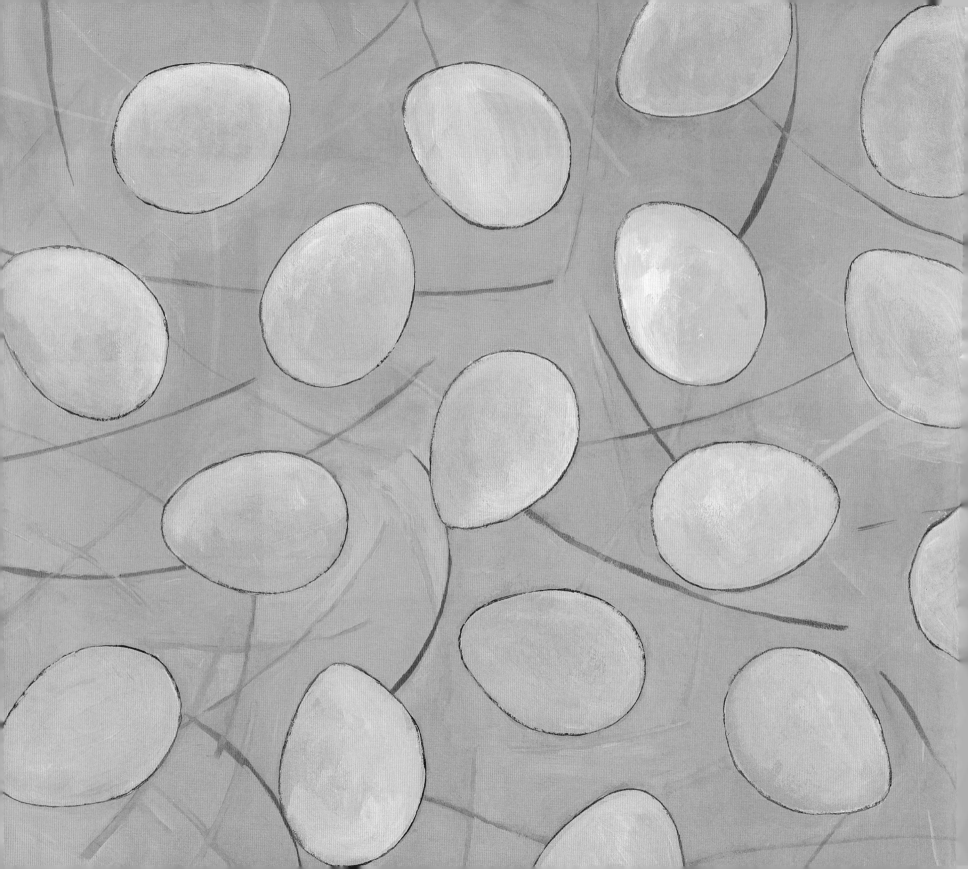

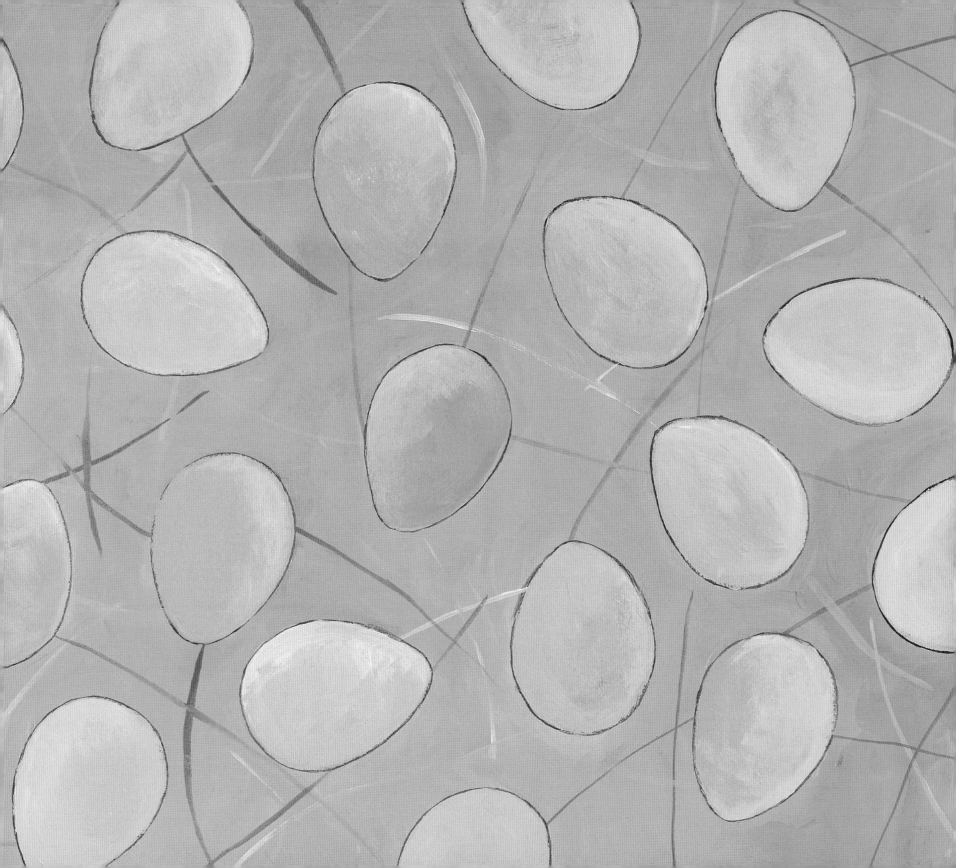

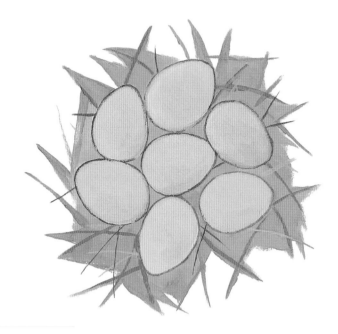

For Timothy and the North
Hampshire Hospital
Special Care Baby Unit
~ J S

For Emily Anna
~ J C

LITTLE TIGER PRESS
1 The Coda Centre, 189 Munster Road, London SW6 6AW
www.littletiger.co.uk

First published in Great Britain 1997
This edition published 2014 by Little Tiger Press, London
Text copyright © Julie Sykes 1997
Illustrations copyright © Jane Chapman 1997
Visit Jane Chapman at www.ChapmanandWarnes.com
Julie Sykes and Jane Chapman have asserted their rights to be
identified as the author and illustrator of this work under the
Copyright, Designs and Patents Act, 1988

All rights reserved • ISBN 978-1-84895-850-0

Printed in China • LTP/1900/0818/1013
2 4 6 8 10 9 7 5 3 1

DORA'S EGGS

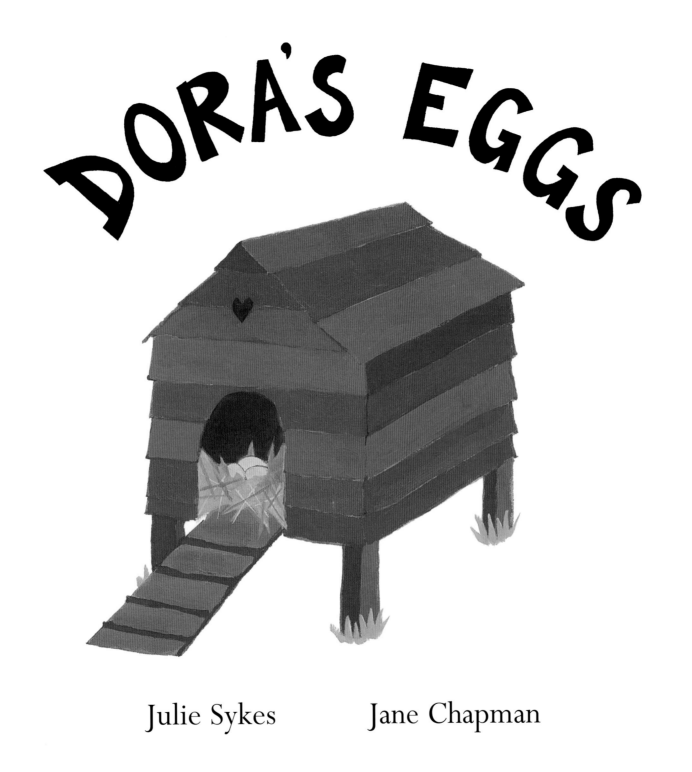

Julie Sykes   Jane Chapman

LITTLE TIGER PRESS

Dora was sitting on a nest of eggs.
They were shiny brown and smooth
to touch.

"These are my very first eggs,"
clucked Dora proudly.
"I would like all my friends to
come and admire them."

Dora climbed out of the hen house
and into the farmyard.
"Who shall I visit first?" she asked.
"I know! I'll find Debbie Duck."

Dora hopped over the fence and across the field
until she reached the pond.
"Hello, Debbie," called Dora. "Would you like
to come and see my eggs?"
"I can't come now," quacked Debbie. "I'm teaching
my babies to swim."

Dora stood watching the ducklings
splashing around and learning to paddle.
Somehow she felt a bit less excited.
"My eggs are nice," she thought.
"But those fluffy ducklings are
much nicer."

Dora felt just a little sad as she trotted off to the
sty to visit Penny Pig.

"Hello, Penny," she clucked. "Would you like to come
and see my eggs?"

But Penny didn't hear. She was having too much fun,
tumbling around with her wriggly piglets.

Dora sighed.
"My eggs are nice," she said. "But those
wriggly piglets are much nicer."

Dora sighed again as she climbed the hill to find
Sally Sheep. "Would you like to come and see
my eggs?" she asked Sally.
"Not today," bleated Sally. "I'm too busy keeping
an eye on my lambs."

Dora looked at the lambs, frolicking in the field. She felt even sadder. "My eggs are nice," she thought. "But those playful lambs are much nicer."

Very slowly, Dora walked back to the farmyard.
On her way she bumped into Daisy Dog.
"Hello, Daisy," clucked Dora. "Would you like
to come and see my eggs?"
"Sorry, Dora," barked Daisy, wagging her tail.
"I can't come now. I'm taking my puppies
for a walk."

Dora was beginning to feel
quite miserable.
"My eggs are nice," she said.
"But those puppies out
for a walk are much nicer."

In the farmyard Dora stopped
at the cowshed. She wished she
felt happier, but perhaps Clarissa
the Cow would cheer her up.
"Would you like to see my eggs?"
she called.

"Sssh," mooed Clarissa softly, nodding her head at
the straw. Snuggled up by her feet and fast asleep
was a newborn calf. Dora felt like crying.
"My eggs are nice," she whispered. "But that little
calf, all snuggled up, is much nicer."

Dora walked back across the yard in the
sunlight and climbed into the hen house.
Her eggs were just as she had left them,
smooth and brown and very still.
"My eggs are nice," sighed Dora, fluffing
out her feathers. "But everyone else's
babies are *much* nicer."

Very sadly, Dora settled
herself down onto
her nest . . .

CRACK!

Dora jumped up in surprise.

"Oh, no!" cried Dora. "I've broken them!"
Tears began to roll down her face.
They splashed onto the nest and over
the cracked eggs. As each tear fell,
the cracks grew wider and wider until
suddenly . . .

. . . up popped a fluffy head,
then another, and another.

Soon the nest was full of tiny
chicks.
"Cheep, cheep," the chicks
squeaked. "Cheep, cheep."
Dora stopped crying and stared.

It didn't matter that the eggs were broken.
The new chicks were everything Dora
had ever wanted!

Proudly she strutted out into the farmyard,
and one by one the chicks followed after her.
All the animals stopped and stared.

"Oh, Dora!" quacked Debbie.

"They're as fluffy as my ducklings!"

"And wriggly like my piglets,"
oinked Penny.

"They're as playful as my lambs,"
baaed Sally.

"And you can take them for walks—
just like my puppies," barked Daisy.

"But best of all," mooed Clarissa,

"your chicks can snuggle up to you,
like my calf snuggles up to me."

"Cluck," said Dora happily, agreeing
with her friends. "My eggs were nice,
but my chicks are much, much nicer!"

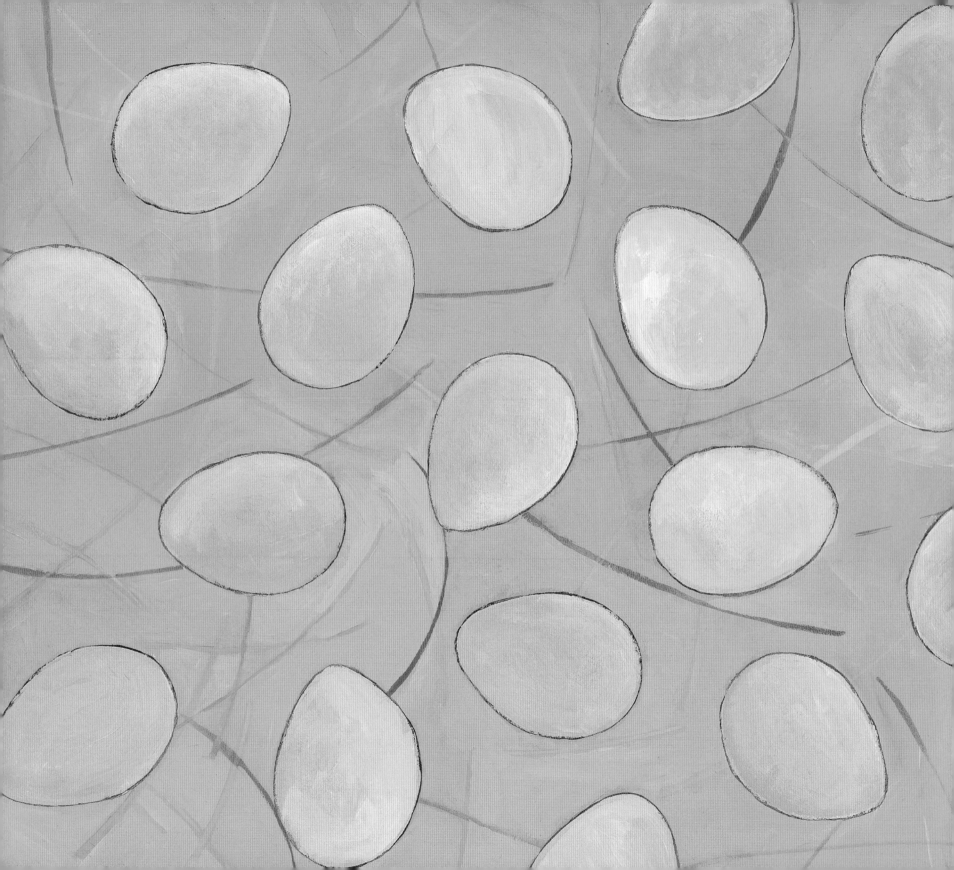